GOODNIGHT MOON

by Margaret Wise Brown
Pictures by Clement Hurd

HARPERCOLLINS*PUBLISHERS*

Copyright 1947 by Harper & Row, Publishers, Inc.
Text copyright renewed 1975 by Roberta Brown Rauch
Illustrations copyright renewed 1975 by Edith T. Hurd, Clement Hurd,
John Thacher Hurd, and George Hellyer,
as Trustees of the Edith and Clement Hurd 1982 Trust.
Printed in the United States of America.
ISBN-10: 0-06-077585-8 (trade bdg.)—ISBN-13: 978-0-06-077585-8 (trade bdg.)
ISBN-10: 0-06-077586-6 (lib. bdg.)—ISBN-13: 978-0-06-077586-5 (lib. bdg.)
ISBN-10: 0-06-443017-0 (pbk.)—ISBN-13: 978-0-06-443017-3 (pbk.)
Revised edition, 2005.
For information address HarperCollins Children's Books, a division of HarperCollins Publishers,
10 East 53rd Street, New York, NY 10022.
www.harperchildrens.com
09 10 11 12 13 WOR 20

In the great green room
There was a telephone
And a red balloon
And a picture of—

The cow jumping over the moon

And there were three little bears sitting on chairs

And two little kittens
And a pair of mittens

And a little toyhouse
And a young mouse

And a comb and a brush and a bowl full of mush

And a quiet old lady who was whispering "hush"

Goodnight room

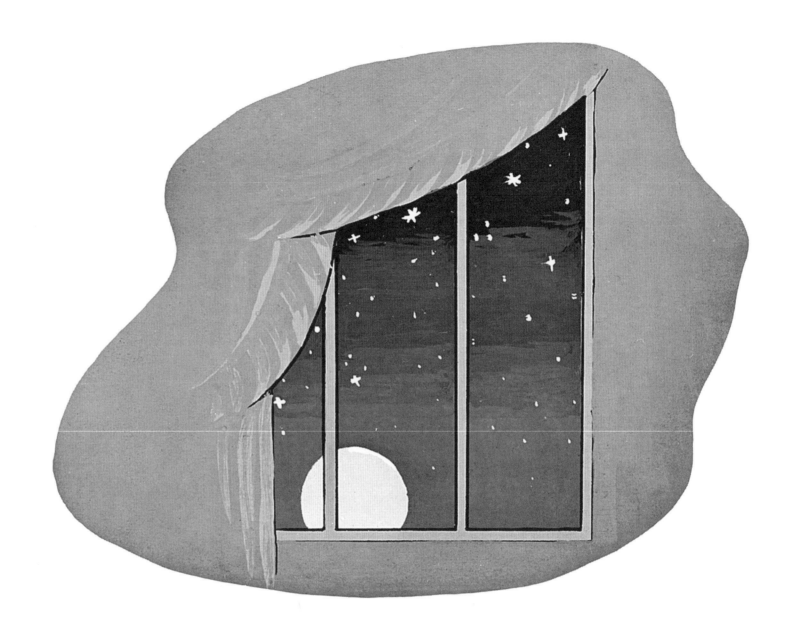

Goodnight moon

Goodnight cow jumping over the moon

Goodnight light
And the red balloon

Goodnight bears
Goodnight chairs

Goodnight kittens

And goodnight mittens

Goodnight clocks
And goodnight socks

Goodnight little house

And goodnight mouse

Goodnight comb
And goodnight brush

Goodnight nobody

Goodnight mush

And goodnight to the old lady
whispering "hush"

Goodnight stars

Goodnight air

Goodnight noises everywhere